Many educators now believe that children as young as three years of age can learn to recognize and read words. Your young child can learn to do so with this EARLY-START Preschool Reader. It tells a story about an everyday situation familiar to all children. Only 50 different words are used to tell the story. These are repeated throughout the book, so that the child soon learns to recognize them and to understand their meaning.

The 50 words in this book are:

elevators	waking	squirrels	come	land
up	until	see	crack	is
airplanes	they	long	pigeons	comes
blast	go	swinging	run	ball
it	down	it's	sun	fly
on	take	lie	people	you
into	the	going	walking	all
and	will	balloons	night	are
can	moon	off	goes	reaching
day	glove	rocket	float	then

Read this book through with your child a few times. Answer any questions that he asks about the words in the story. After two or three such readings, he will begin to show interest in reading the book by himself.

Up and Down

by Maggie Jardine

illustrated by Richard C. Lewis

WONDER BOOKS • NEW YORK
A Division of GROSSET & DUNLAP, Inc.

Copyright © 1965

Initial Teaching Alphabet Publications, Inc.
Publishers of Educational Materials in Pitman's i|t|a
20 East 46 Street, New York City, N. Y. 10017

All rights reserved. No part of this book
may be reproduced in any form without
the written permission of the publisher.

Printed in the United States of America
P-987654321

This popularly priced edition is a reprint in the traditional alphabet of a book originally published for schools in Pitman's Initial Teaching Alphabet.

Consultants:

Albert J. Mazurkiewicz, Ed.D.
Lehigh University

Harold J. Tanyzer, Ph.D.
Hofstra University

Elevators go down.

Balloons float down.

Airplanes take off.

Airplanes land.

Blast off!
The rocket
is going up!

It will come down
on the moon.

It comes down into the glove.

Pigeons fly up,

Squirrels run up,

You can see the sun come up.

You can see the sun go down.

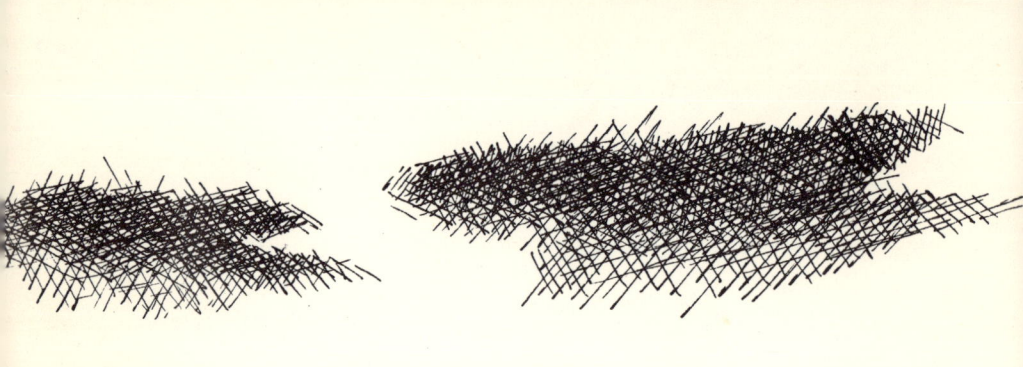

and swinging up

and reaching up

until it's night, and then

they all lie down.